Keisha's Doors

An Autism Story—Book One

Las Puertas de Keisha

Una Historia de Autismo—Libro Uno

Written by / Escrita por

Marvie Ellis

Illustrated by / Ilustrada por

Jenny Loehr

Disclaimer

This story herein is based on the author's extensive experience and knowledge. Readers should not attempt these therapy techniques without the supervision of, advice and training by qualified professionals.

Rectificación

Esta historia está basada en la extensa experiencia y conocimientos de la autora. Los amables lectores no deben de emprender estas técnica de terapia sin la supervisión, consejo y entrenamiento de profesionales expertos.

Published in 2005 by Speech Kids Texas Press, Inc.,
301 Hesters Crossing Road, Suite 120,
Round Rock, Texas 78681.

ISBN: (1-933319-00-3) hardback
Library of Congress Card Number: 2005901419

Ellis, Marvie
Keisha's Doors / written by Marvie Ellis; illustrated by Jenny Loehr.
1 st. ed. - Round Rock, Texas.:
Speech Kids Texas Press, Inc., © 2005.
32 p.: col. Ill.; 29 cm.
An Autism Story
Summary: An older sister can't understand why her little sister, Keisha, won't play with her. The family finds out that Keisha has autism and goes to see a therapist to understand what autism means to them.
1. Autism- Juvenile fiction. 2. Siblings- Juvenile fiction. 3. Sensory- Juvenile fiction.
4. Therapist- Juvenile fiction. 5. African-American- Juvenile Fiction.
6. Spanish Translation- Juvenile Fiction. 1. Loehr, Jenny, ill. II. Title.
First Edition. Text copyright © 2005 by Marvie Ellis.
Illustrations copyright © 2005 by Jenny Loehr.

For inquiries about the author and information about
Speech Kids Texas Press, Inc., please visit our website at

www.speechkidstexaspress.com

Rita Mills—Book Packaging Consultant—The Book Connection
Cindy Guire—Cover Design

The paper used in this publication meets the requirements of the American National Standard for Permanence of Paper for Printed Library Materials Z39.48-1984.
Printed in Hong Kong

Acknowledgements

Thank you my husband, Tellis and son, Brian for your love, support and patience. I love you very much.

Thank you my mentor / sister / friend, Karla Frazier, D.M.D., in Austin for your tremendous encouragement and my bright teeth (www.the2thdoctor.com).
Thank you my sister, Lynn Harris and family for letting me read to you over the phone past bedtime.
Thank you my brother, Calvin Frazier, for being a great soundboard.
Thank you Mom (Mrs. Marvie Frazier) for without whom none of my business dreams could have been.
Thank you, Grandmas Tommie & MaMas, Grandpa Georgie, and my father-in-law, T.B. Ellis, III, M.D., for your daily prayers and encouragement.
Thank you, Dolly for your editing skills.
Thank you, Mrs. Maria L. Cruz for translating the stories.
Thank you, Jenny for having a special gift and sharing it with me. Thank you, Lavelle Carlson for being a role model.
Thank you, Rita Mills for your time, advice and contributions.
Thank you my wonderful and gifted staff at Speech Kids, P.C. for your support and patience.
Thanks to all the parents and professionals who took the time and care to review the stories.

Most of all, thank you to all the children with ASD, you are most inspiring.

May God bless and keep us.

Foreword

This collection of stories is a reflection of the importance of understanding the diversity of individuals with autism. In this ground-breaking series, many nuances of autism are explored. Perspectives from parents and siblings are provided. These heart warming short stories are useful for anyone who interacts with those with autism.

This is the first time a series of books has been presented specifically on autism in a short, easy to read, and dual language format. The format allows for quick reading with just enough information to spark the desire for further exploration. These books are beneficial to anyone who deals with individuals who have autism of any age. They can be useful for teachers, day care providers, students, medical professionals, psychologists, occupational therapists, physical therapists, speech-language pathologists, administrators, ministers, bus drivers, etc. People with autism are becoming more involved in the community, and the importance of a basic understanding, or at least some familiarity with this condition is necessary.

It is my hope, that this series of books is just the beginning of a whole new wave of consciousness as it relates to individuals with disabilities. It is so rewarding to see a series of stories that is so beneficial to many people, yet simple enough to facilitate basic understanding of such a complex condition. The inclusion of therapeutic techniques offers a unique and indirect perspective of the many facets of autism. These stories are definitely worth reading.

LaQuinta Khaldun, M.S., CCC-SLP
Speech-Language Pathologist/ Owner
Carolina Speech Services
Charlotte, NC

Keisha's Doors

Las Puertas de Keisha

Sometimes I wonder why my little sister,
Keisha, won't play with me. Keisha is almost
three years old. I am her big sister, Monica,
and I am nine and a half years old.

A veces pienso porqué mi hermana menor,
Keisha, no juega conmigo. Keisha tiene tres
años de edad. Yo soy su hermana mayor,
Mónica, y yo tengo nueve años y medio.

When I bring out blocks and dolls for us to play, Keisha will pick them up, throw them down, and walk away. She doesn't seem to know how to play with toys.

Cuando saco bloques y muñecas para jugar, Keisha los coje, los tira al suelo, y se va. Parece que no sabe como jugar con jugetes.

She used to say a few words like, "mama," "dada," and "bye-bye." But, she stopped talking before she turned two years old. Keisha doesn't seem to listen or look up when we talk to her.

Ella decía unas cuantas palabras como, "mamá," "papá," y "adios." Pero dejo de hablar cuando cumplio dos años. Parece que Keisha no oye y no te mira cuando le hablas.

When Mom asks Keisha to say a word, she walks
away and rocks on her
pink rocking chair.

Cuando mi mamá le pide a Keisha que diga una
palabra, ella se va a su mecedora rosa y se mece.

Keisha loves to rock back and forth. One time,
when her rocking chair broke,
Keisha rocked on her bed
until Dad bought her a
new rocking chair that
looked exactly like
the old one.

Le gusta a Keisha mecerse. En una ocasión cuando su mecedora
se quebró, Keisha se meció en su cama hasta que papá le
compró una mecedora nueva exactamente igual que su
mecedora vieja.

Mom and Dad took Keisha to see
some special doctors at the hospital.
It took a long time for the
doctors to talk with my
parents and to test Keisha.

Mamá y papá llevaron a Keisha a ver
doctores especialistas en el hospital.
Pasó mucho tiempo en hacer los
examenes y en las platicas de los
doctores con mis padres.

The doctors asked my parents
what favorite foods Keisha
liked to eat. They were
not surprised to hear
that she was a
picky eater.

Drumstick

Chicken Nuggets

Apple Juice

Dry Cereal

Fruit

Vegetables

Pasta

Burger

Water

Milk

Los doctores le
preguntaron a mis
padres que era lo que le
gustaba comer a Keisha. No les
sorprendió saber que no le gustaba comer.

After a
while,
the doctors
told my parents
that Keisha was
autistic. Mom and
Dad had never
heard of
autism before
and neither had I.

Después de
un tiempo los
doctores les
dijeron a mis
padres que
Keisha es
autística. Mi
mamá, papá y
yo nunca
habíamos sabido
de austimo.

The doctors said it meant Keisha would need a lot of extra help
learning to listen, learn, play, and talk.
They wanted Keisha to go see
a therapist because
that person could
help Keisha with
her learning.

Los doctores dijeron que esto significaba que Keisha necesitaría
mucha ayuda para aprender a escuchar, estudiar, jugar, y hablar.
Querían que Keisha consultara con una terapeuta porque le
ayudaría a Keisha a aprender.

My parents took Keisha to see
Ms. Sheri at the Therapy Center.
She played with her and spoke to
my parents for a couple of hours.

Mis padres llevaron a Keisha a
consultar con la Sra. Sheri en el
Centro del Terapia. Ella jugó con
ella y habló con mis padres
por un par de horas.

We were still having trouble understanding what it meant to be autistic. Ms. Sheri said that inside of Keisha are some inner doors that shut out parts of her surroundings.

Todavía es difícil entender lo que es autismo. La Sra. Sheri dice que Keisha tiene unas puertas interiores que bloquean parte de sus alrededores.

These doors are closed to playing
with and talking to family
and friends, learning
how to listen
and follow
directions,
and being
aware of
people
around her.

Estas puertas están cerradas cuando quiere
jugar y platicar con la familia y amistades,
para aprender a escuchar y entender
instrucciones, y darse cuenta de
las personas
que la
rodean.

Ms. Sheri said she would teach us how
to help Keisha open her inner
doors. She started teaching
us some sign language.
Then she taught us
what she
called "open
door ideas."

play

jugar

La Sra. Sheri nos dijo que nos enseñaría como ayudar
a Keisha para que pueda abrir sus puertas interiores.
Ella principió a enseñarnos lenguaje de señales. Ella también
nos enseñó lo que ella llama "ideas para abrir puertas."

One idea was called "face-to-face." Ms. Sheri
said we should bend our knees
and get face level with
Keisha when we
spoke to her.

Una idea se llama "cara a cara."
La Sra. Sheri nos dijo que doblaramos
nuestras rodillas, y vieramos a Keisha a la cara cuando
hablaramos con ella.

She said it
was like
standing at
her front
doorway
saying,
"Here I am,
please let
me in."

Ella nos dijo
que era como si
estuvieramos
enfrente de su
puerta principal
diciendo, "Aqui
estoy, dejame
entrar por favor."

Another idea was called "hands-to-face." To do this, we take Keisha's hands and put them on our cheeks when we talk to her.

Otra idea se llama "manos a cara."
Para hacer esto, tomamos las manos de Keisha y la ponemos sobre nuestras mejillas cuando hablamos con ella.

Ms. Sheri said that touch makes Keisha
more aware that we are
there and hopefully
will make her want
to open a door.

La Sra. Sheri
dijo que al
tocarla, Keisha
siente que
estamos con
ella y
robablemente
ella abra la
puerta.

She let us practice "face-to-face" and "hands-to-face" with her. Then, she asked my parents to try it with Keisha at home for the next few weeks.

Ella nos permitió practicar "cara a cara" y "manos a cara" con ella. Después les pidió a mis padres que lo hiceran con Keisha en cas a por unas cuantas semanas.

Mom was a little worried because this was a
new way to talk to her. One
day at home, Mom bent
down to Keisha's face.

Mamá estaba preocupada porque esta es
una manera nueva de platicar con ella.
Un dia en casa mi mamá se agachó y miró a Keisha en su cara.

She took Keisha's hands and put them
to her cheeks. Mom
looked at Keisha
and said,
"Hi baby."

Tomó las manos de Keisha y las puso en sus mejillas.
Mamá miro a Keisha y le dijo, "Hola bebé."

Instead of ignoring Mom or turning away, Keisha did something new. She lifted her head, looked at Mom, and said in a soft voice, "Hi."

En lugar de ignorar a mamá o irse, Keisha hizo algo nuevo. Levantó la cabeza, miró a mamá, y dijo en voz baja, "Hola."

We were all so happy! I saw tears
running down Mom's cheeks.

Estabamos tan contentos! Ví
que se derramaban las lagrimas
en las mejilla de mi mamá.

We took Keisha to see Ms. Sheri the following week. She said she believed Keisha's doors were beginning to open.

Llevamos a Keisha a ver la Sra. Sheri la semana siguiente. Ella nos dijo que creía que las puertas de Keisha principiaban a abrirse.

Ms. Sheri said there will be many days that Keisha won't say words when we want her to. But, with lots of therapy, Keisha will open all her doors and welcome us in.

La Sra. Sheri nos dijo que muchas veces Keisha no va a decir las palabras que nosotros queremos que diga. Pero, con mucha terapia, Keisha abrirá sus puertas y nos dará la bienvenida.

Parent Reviews

"I LOVED your stories...I learned some new techniques . . . If I had a child with more severe autism, this story would send me straight to his speech therapist asking about these. . . ."
—*Michelle S. (son with ASD)*

"This is a beautiful story (and my favorite). I appreciated the way you described Keisha's 'disconnection' as being 'inner doors that shut out certain surroundings.' I also like the 'open door ideas' as a means to reach Keisha. I believe that this story is perfect for parents, siblings and anyone else who needs an understanding of what it's like as an autistic child and better yet, what we can do to try and enter their world."
—*Lisa B. (son with ASD)*

"We found our children in the story as they were in their own world with their 'invisible secret doors.'"
—*Cuc N. (daughter & son with ASD)*

"Marvie's series of books really hit home for us. They will benefit anyone who loves someone on the spectrum. These stories give explanations to help understanding and encourage interaction. Hats off to you, Marvie!"
—*Paul & Stacey S.*
(son who was recently diagnosed out of ASD)
Hooray!

Comentarios de Padres de Familia

"AMO sus historias...Aprendí técnicas nuevas...Si tuviera un niño con autismo más severo, esta historia me llevaría inmediatamente a un patólogo de la lengua para pedirlas . . . ."
—*Michelle S. (hijo tiene ASD.)*

"Esta es una bella historia (y mi favorita). Aprecio la manera en que describió la 'desconección' de Keisha como "puertas internas que bloquean ciertos alrededores.' También me gustan las ideas de 'abrir puertas' para allegarse a Keisha. Creo que esta historia es perfecta para padres, hermanos y cualquier persona que necesita entender la vida de un niño autista y lo mejor es, lo que podemos hacer para entrar en su mundo.'"
—*Lisa B. (hijo tiene ASD)*

"Encontramos a nuestors hijos en esta historia como viven en su propio mundo con sus 'puertas invisibles y secretas.'"
—*Cuc N. (hija e hijo tienen ASD)*

"Las series de libros de Marvie tienen mucho impacto para nosotros. Beneficiarán mucho a las personas que aman a alguien en el espectro. Estas historias dan explicaciones para ayudar a enteneder y para animar a interacción. Bien hecho, Marvie!"
—*Paul & Stacey S. (tienen un hijo que recientemente salió de ASD) bravo!*

Professional Reviews

"The stories are great....They are clever and intriguing."
—*Chris P. Johnson, M.Ed., M.D., American Academy of Pediatrics (AAP) Committee on Children with Disabilities and Co-chair of the AAP Autism Expert Panel; Clinical Professor of Pediatrics at the Health Science Center at the University of Texas at San Antonio Founder of CAMP (the Children's Association for Maximal Potential)*

"In this story, the analogy of open doors and shut doors is used to explain the difficulties in sensory reception in children with autism. The . . . strategy of using alternative sensory channels to compensate for the poorly functioning auditory channel is very helpful in explaining how to communicate with children who cannot communicate in a typical manner."
—*Kapila Seshadri, M.D., Associate Professor of Pediatrics, Section Head, Section of NeuroDevelopmental Disabilities, Department of Pediatrics, UMDNJ—Robert Wood Johnson Medical School, New Jersey*

"[This story] for family members [was] delightful. I feel [it] would be very beneficial for young family members who are struggling to understand autism."
– *Barbara A. Booth, Ph.D., BCBA, Director of Special Education, Pflugerville, Texas ISD*

"I would definitely consider them for purchase as there seems to be a paucity of books to read to young children...Thanks again for making the effort to supply a need."
—*Janne Zochert, Education Coordinator, Head Start, Williamson-Burnet County, Texas*

"This story is beautifully told from a sibling's point of view. This is a great way to understand how autism affects other children in the family. It offers some insight into the beginning stages of basic techniques that are family friendly. The 'door' concept is a nice way to explain what it is like for those with autism as well as those who interact with them."

—*LaQuinta Khaldun, M.S., CCC-SLP,*
owner of Carolina Speech Services, North Carolina.

"A heartfelt story from the perspective of an older sibling of a child with autism. It describes one family's journey through the diagnosis and understanding of autism, as well as ways to 'connect' with this child. This story is appropriate for siblings, peers, and families that are going through this journey. I feel it gives hope to families that are currently going through the confusing and often frightening time of diagnosis and discovery."

—*Hope Korbet, M.S., CCC-SLP,*
Kennedy Krieger Institute, Center for Autism
and Related Disorders, Baltimore, MD.

Comentarios Profesionales

"Las historias son muy buenas . . . . Son ingeniosas e intrigantes."

—*Chris P. Johnson, M.Ed., M.D.,*
Academia Americana de Pediatría (AAP) Comite para
Niños Deshabilitados y co-presidente del Jurado
Experto en Autismo; Profesor de la Clínica en Pediatría
del Centro de Ciencias Médicas en la Universidad de
Texas de San Antonio, y miembro fundador de CAMP
(the Children's Association for Maximal Potential – la
Asociacion de Potencial Máximo Para Niños)

"En esta historia, la analogía de abrir y cerrar puertas es usada para explicar las dificultades de recepción sensorial en niños con autismo. La estrategia de usar canales sensoriales alternos para compensar los canales auditorios que no trabajan bien es muy útil para explicar como comunicarse con niños que no pueden comunicarse de una manera común."

—*Kapila Seshadri, M.D., Profesor Asociado de*
Pediatría, Director de Sección, Sección de
Deshabilidades de NeuroDesarrollo, Departamento
de Pediatría, UMDNJ—Robert Wood
Johnson Medical School, New Jersey

"[Esta historia] para miembros de la familia es encantadora. Creo que puede beneficiar a los miembros menores de la familia que están batallando para entender autismo."

—*Barbara A. Booth, Ph.D., BCBA,*
Directora de Educación Especial, Distrito Escolar
Independiente de Pflugerville, Texas

"Considero que definitivamente los compraría ya que son libros que se pueden leer con niños pequeños.... De nuevo, gracias por esforzarse en abastecer esta demanda."

—*Janne Zochert, Coordinadora de Educación,*
Head Start, Williamson-Burnet County, Texas

"Esta historia reconoce la realidad multifacética de autismo. Demostrando como se le permite al hermano estar involucrado en la terapia es muy positivo. La historia describe como los hermanos pueden tomar una parte integral en el proceso de comunicación. También demuestra como los hermanos desean aprender y ayudar."

—*LaQuinta Khaldun, M.S., CCC-SLP,*
dueña de Carolina Speech Services, North Carolina

"Una historia que llega al corazón desde el punto de vista de un hemano mayor con un hermano autista. Describe la jornada de la familia desde el diagnóstico hasta el entendimiento de autismo, así como la manera de 'conectar' con este niño. La historia es apropiada para hermanos, amigos y familiares que están haciendo este viaje. Creo que dá esperanzas a las familias que están pasando por el diagnóstico y descubrimiento lo cual es muy confuso y terrible."

—*Hope Korbet, M.S., CCC-SLP, Instituto Kenned*
Krieger, Centro para Autismo y Deshabilidades
Relacionadas con el Autismo, Baltimore, Maryland

About the Author:

Marvie Ellis received her Bachelor of Science degree in Communicative Disorders from Jackson State University in Jackson, Mississippi and her Master of Science degree from the University of North Carolina at Chapel Hill (1996). She has specialized training in working with the birth to five population, children with autism spectrum disorders, speech-language delays, oral motor therapy, play based therapy, sensory therapy, and behavior modification techniques. Marvie also provides trainings and seminars to parents and educators in the Austin surrounding areas. She is a member of the American Speech-Language and Hearing Association, Texas Speech-Language and Hearing Association, and the Autism Society of America. She owns a private pediatric speech-language and occupational therapy practice (Speech Kids, P.C.) in Round Rock, Texas. Marvie lives in Austin with her husband, Tellis and son, Brian. She enjoys writing stories, supporting others in their entrepreneurial endeavors and quiet moments for meditation.

La Autora:

Marvie Ellis obtuvo su Bachillerato en Ciencias en Desórdenes de Comunicación de la Universidad del Estado de Jackson en Jackson, Mississippi y su Maestría en Ciencias de la Universidad de North Carolina en Chapel Hill (1996). Se ha especializado trabajando con niños que tienen desórdenes de autismo, habla y lenguaje retrasado, terapia de motor oral, terapia basada en juegos, terapia sensorial, y técnicas modificando comportamiento de niños desde su nacimiento hasta los cinco años. Marvie también entrena y presenta seminarios para padres y educadores en Austin y sus alrededores. Es miembro de la Asociación Americana de Habla y Lenguaje, Asociación de Texas de Habla-Lenguaje y Oído de la Asociación Americana de Autismo. Es dueña de la Clínica privada, (Speech Kids, P.C.), especializada en habla-lenguaje y terapia ocupacional en Round Rock, Texas. Marvie vive en Austin con su esposo, Tellis e hijo, Brian. Le gusta escribir historias, para ayudar a personas en sus ocupaciones y momentos de meditación.

About the Illustrator:

Jenny Loehr obtained her Master of Arts degree in Speech Pathology in northern California at Humboldt State University in 1990. She has been practicing art and illustration three times as long as she has been a clinician, and recently been able to "marry" the two professions by opening Curly Girl Studios where she illustrates books and materials for the speech-language pathology and audiology community. Jenny spends her days illustrating and practicing speech pathology in Austin, Texas where she lives with her husband Brian, and her two boys, Jacob and Joshua.

La Ilustradora:

Jenny Loehr obtuvo su Maestría de Arte en Patología de Habla en California del Norte en la Universidad del Estado Humboldt en 1990. Ha ejercido su arte como ilustradora tres veces más tiempo que el tiempo que ha ejercido en clínicas, y recientemente ha podido combinar sus dos profesiones en sus Curly Girl Studios, ilustrando libros y documentos para la comunidad especializada en patología de habla-lenguaje y audiología. Jenny pasa sus días ilustrando y practicando patología de habla en Austin, Texas, donde vive con su esposo Brian, y sus dos hijos, Jacob y Joshua.